# Kashtanka

*Translated by Richard Pevear*

# Kashtanka

BY ANTON CHEKHOV

*Designed and illustrated by Barry Moser*

G. P. PUTNAM'S SONS   *New York*

*For Eudora Welty*
*—B.M.*

Translation copyright © 1991 by Richard Pevear
Illustrations copyright © 1991 by Pennyroyal Press, Inc.
All rights reserved. This book, or parts thereof, may not be reproduced in any form without permission in writing from the publisher. G. P. Putnam's Sons, a division of The Putnam & Grosset Book Group, 200 Madison Avenue, New York, NY 10016.
Published simultaneously in Canada.
Printed in Hong Kong by South China Printing Co. (1988) Ltd.
Book design by Barry Moser
Lettering by Reassurance Wunder
Text set in Baskerville

This version of Chekhov's original 1889 text has been translated for young readers.

Library of Congress Cataloging-in-Publication Data
Chekhov, Anton Pavlovich, 1860–1904.
Kashtanka = (Little Chestnut)
Summary: A circus clown adopts Kashtanka the dog
after she becomes separated from her master while out
on a walk.   1. Dogs—Juvenile fiction. [1. Dogs—Fiction.
2. Circus—Fiction] I. Pevear, Richard, 1943–
II. Moser, Barry, ill. III. Title. IV. Title: Little
Chestnut. PZ10.3.c4154Ka   1991   [Fic]   89–10866
ISBN 0–399–21905–6
10 9 8 7 6 5 4 3 2 1
First Impression

# Contents

# Kashtanka

I. *Misbehavior*

A YOUNG, rusty-red dog, half dachshund and half mutt, with the sharp ears and nose of a fox, was running up and down the sidewalk, looking anxiously in all directions. Every once in a while she stopped and whined, shifting from one frozen paw to the other, trying to figure out how she could have gotten lost.

She remembered perfectly well the events of the day that had brought her to this unfamiliar sidewalk.

The day had begun when her master, the cabinetmaker Luka Alexandritch, put on his hat, took some wooden thing under his arm, and hollered, "Kashtanka, let's go!"

Hearing her name, the half-dachshund half-mutt came out from under the workbench where she slept on the wood shavings, stretched happily, and ran after her master.

Luka's customers lived far apart, so on his way from one to the other he had to stop several times at a tavern to fortify himself. Kashtanka remembered that she had behaved very badly. She was so overjoyed to be going for a walk that she jumped about, barked at trolley cars, dashed into backyards, and chased other dogs. The cabinetmaker kept losing sight of her and would stop and shout angrily at her. Once, with a cross

expression on his face, he even grabbed her foxlike ear in his fist, shook her, and said slowly and firmly, "You . . . are . . . a . . . little . . . pest!"

Having seen his customers, Luka had stopped at his sister's, where he had a bite to eat and a few more drinks. From his sister's, he went to see a bookbinder he knew; from the bookbinder's, he went to a tavern; from the tavern to another friend's house, and so on. In short, by the time Kashtanka found herself on the unfamiliar sidewalk, it was getting dark and the cabinetmaker was as drunk as a fish. He waved his arms and moaned, "I'm a sinner! Oh, what a sinner I am . . . !"

Then, lowering his voice, he had called Kashtanka and told her, "You, Kashtanka, are a bug, a flea, nothing more. Compared to a man, you're like a carpenter compared to a cabinetmaker. . . . "

Suddenly there had come a burst of music. Kashtanka looked around and saw a regiment of soldiers marching down the street straight at her. She couldn't stand music, which made her nervous, and she rushed around and howled. But to her great surprise, the cabinetmaker wasn't frightened at all. Instead of yelping and barking, he grinned broadly, stood at attention, and gave a salute. Seeing that her master did not protest, Kashtanka howled even louder, then lost her head and ran to the other side of the street.

When she came to her senses, the music had already stopped and the regiment was gone. She rushed back across the street, but alas, the cabinetmaker was also gone. Kashtanka began sniffing the sidewalk, hoping to find her master by the smell of his tracks. But some scoundrel had just walked past in new galoshes, and now all the delicate scents were mixed

with the strong smell of rubber, so that it was impossible to tell one from the other.

Kashtanka ran here and there but could not find her master. Meanwhile night was falling. The lamps were lighted on both sides of the street, and lights appeared in the windows. Big, fluffy snowflakes were falling, painting the sidewalks, the horses' backs, and the coachmen's hats white, and the darker it grew, the whiter everything became.

Fear and despair overcame Kashtanka. She was tired from her long day's travels with Luka, her ears and paws were cold, and she was terribly hungry. Only twice in the whole day had she had anything to eat: at the bookbinder's she had lapped up some paste, and in one of the taverns she had found a sausage skin near the counter—that was all. She huddled in a doorway and began whining piteously.

## II. *A Mysterious Stranger*

When soft, fluffy snow had completely covered Kashtanka's back and head, and she had sunk into a deep slumber from exhaustion, suddenly the door clicked, creaked, and hit her on the side. She jumped up. A man came out, and as Kashtanka squealed and got under his feet, he could not help noticing her.

The man leaned down and asked, "Where did you come from, little dog? Did I hurt you? Poor thing, poor thing. . . . Don't be angry. . . . It was my fault."

Kashtanka looked up at the stranger through the snowflakes that stuck to her eyelashes and saw a short, fat little man

with a round, clean-shaven face, wearing a top hat and an unbuttoned fur coat.

"Why are you whining?" the man went on, brushing the snow from her back. "Where is your master? Are you lost? Oh, poor little dog! What shall we do now?"

Catching a warm, friendly note in the stranger's voice, Kashtanka licked his hand and whined even more pitifully.

"Well, aren't you a cute one!" said the stranger. "A real little fox! I guess I don't have much choice, do I? Come on, then, maybe I'll find some use for you. . . ."

He whistled and made a sign with his hand which for Kashtanka could mean only one thing: "Let's go!" Kashtanka went.

In less than half an hour she was sitting on the floor of a large, bright room, with her head cocked, looking tenderly and curiously at the stranger, who was sitting at the table eating supper. He tossed her some scraps as he ate, and she was so hungry that she gobbled them down without tasting anything.

"Your master doesn't feed you very well," said the stranger. "Look how scrawny you are! Just skin and bones. . . !"

Kashtanka ate a lot, yet she didn't feel full, only groggy. After supper she sprawled in the middle of the room, stretched her legs and, feeling pleasantly weary all over, began wagging her tail. While her new master sat back in an armchair, smoking a cigar, she kept trying to decide where she liked it better—at this stranger's or at the cabinetmaker's. At the stranger's everything was poor and ugly. Apart from the armchairs, the sofa, the lamp, and the rugs, he had nothing, and the room seemed empty. At the cabinetmaker's, the whole place was full of interesting things: he had a table, a workbench, a pile of wood shavings, planes, chisels, saws, a basin, a goldfinch in a cage. . . .

15

The stranger's room had no particular smell, while at the cabinetmaker's there was always a cloud of sawdust in the air and the wonderful smell of glue, varnish, and wood shavings. Still, being with the stranger had one great advantage: he gave her a lot to eat. And when she sat by the table with a meek look on her face, he never once hit her or stamped his foot or shouted: "Get out of here, you mutt!"

When he finished his cigar, her new master went out and came back a moment later carrying a small mattress.

"Come here, little dog!" he said, putting the mattress in the corner near the sofa. "Lie down! Go to sleep!"

Then he turned off the lamp and went out. Kashtanka lay down on the mattress and closed her eyes. She heard barking outside and wanted to answer it, but suddenly she became terribly sad. She remembered Luka Alexandritch, his son Fedyushka, and her cozy place under the workbench. . . . She remembered how on long winter evenings while the cabinetmaker was planing a board or reading the newspaper aloud, Fedyushka used to play with her. He would drag her from under the workbench by her hind legs and do such tricks with her that everything turned green in her eyes and all her joints hurt. He would make her walk on her hind legs, turn her into a bell by pulling her tail until she barked, or give her tobacco to sniff. And the more vivid her memories became, the more loudly and longingly Kashtanka whined.

But weariness and warmth soon overcame her longing. . . . She began to fall asleep. In her mind's eye dogs ran past, among them a shaggy old poodle she had seen that day in the street. Fedyushka was chasing the poodle with a chisel in his hand; then all at once he too was covered with shaggy fur, and barked merrily next to Kashtanka. Kashtanka and he sniffed each other's noses good-naturedly and ran off down the street. . . .

## III. *New and Very Pleasant Acquaintances*

It was already light when Kashtanka woke up. There was nobody in the room. Kashtanka stretched, yawned, and began nosing around in a grumpy mood. She sniffed the corners and the furniture, glanced into the entryway and found nothing interesting. Besides the door to the entryway, there was one other door. Kashtanka thought for a moment, then scratched at the door with both paws, opened it, and went into the next room. There on the bed, under a flannel blanket, a man lay sleeping. She recognized him as last night's stranger.

"Grrr. . . ," she growled. Then, remembering yesterday's supper, she wagged her tail and began sniffing.

She sniffed the stranger's clothes and boots and found that they smelled strongly of horse. In the bedroom was another door, also closed. Kashtanka scratched at this door, too, then leaned her chest against it, opened it, and was immediately aware of a very strange, suspicious smell. Sensing trouble, she growled, went cautiously into a small room with dirty wallpaper, and at once drew back in fear. A gray goose, with its head and neck low to the floor and its wings outstretched, was coming straight at her, hissing. Nearby, on a little mat, lay a white tomcat. Seeing Kashtanka, he jumped up, arched his

17

back, lashed his tail, and with his fur standing on end, he too hissed at her. Frightened, but not wanting to show it, Kashtanka barked loudly and rushed at the cat. The cat arched his back even more, hissed, and smacked the dog on the head with his paw. Kashtanka jumped back, crouched down on all fours and, facing the cat, let out a burst of shrill barking. The goose, meanwhile, came from behind and pecked her painfully on the back. Kashtanka jumped up and lunged at the goose.

"What's going on!" shouted an angry voice, and into the room came the stranger, wearing a robe, with a cigar between his teeth. "What's the meaning of all this? Go to your places!"

He went up to the cat, gave him a flick on his arched back, and said, "Fyodor Timofeyitch, what's the meaning of this? You started a fight, eh? You old rapscallion! Lie down!"

And turning to the goose, he shouted, "Ivan Ivanitch, to your place!"

The cat obediently lay down on his mat and closed his eyes. From the look on his face, he seemed ashamed of losing his temper and getting into a fight. Kashtanka whined, offended, and the goose stretched his neck and began explaining something quickly, urgently, distinctly, but quite nonsensically.

"All right, all right," said his master, yawning. "One must live in peace and friendship." He patted Kashtanka and said, "Don't be afraid, rusty. . . . They're nice folks, they won't hurt you. What are we going to call you, anyway? You can't go around without a name, you know."

The stranger thought for a moment, and then said, "I've got it! We'll call you Auntie! Understand. . . ? Auntie!"

And having repeated the word "Auntie" several times, he went out. Kashtanka sat down and kept her eyes open. The cat lay still on his mat, pretending to sleep. The goose stretched his

19

neck and stamped his feet, and went on talking. Apparently he was a very smart goose. After each long harangue, he would step back with a look of amazement as if he were delighted by his own speech. Kashtanka listened to him for a while, answered him with a "grrr," and began sniffing around the corners of the room.

## IV. *Feats of Wonder*

After a while, the stranger came back in carrying an odd thing that looked like a sawhorse. A bell hung from the crosspiece, and there was also a pistol tied to it. Strings were tied to the clapper of the bell and the trigger of the pistol. The stranger set the sawhorse down in the middle of the room. Then he turned to the goose and said, "Ivan, front and center!"

The goose came up to him and stood with a look of anticipation.

"All right," said the stranger, "let's start from the very beginning. First, bow and make a curtsy."

Ivan stretched his neck, nodded his head all around, and scraped the floor with his foot.

"Good boy. . . . Now, play dead!"

The goose turned on his back with his feet sticking up in the air. After a few more simple tricks of this sort, the stranger suddenly clutched his head with an expression of horror and cried, "Fire! Help! The house is burning!"

Ivan ran to the sawhorse, took the string in his beak, and rang the bell.

21

The stranger was very pleased. He stroked the goose's neck and said, "Good boy, Ivan! Now, imagine that you're a jeweler, and you come to your shop one day and find robbers there. What would you do in that case?"

The goose took the other string in his beak and pulled. A loud shot rang out. Kashtanka, who had liked the bell-ringing very much, got so excited by the pistol shot that she ran around the sawhorse barking.

"Auntie, sit!" the stranger shouted. "No barking!"

The shooting was not the end of Ivan's workout. For a whole hour more, the stranger drove the goose around him on a tether, cracking his whip. The goose had to leap over a hurdle, jump through a hoop, and rear up on his tail with his feet waving in the air. Kashtanka couldn't keep her eyes off of Ivan. She howled with delight, and several times started to run after him, yelping. Having worn out the goose and himself as well, the stranger mopped his brow and shouted, "Marya, tell Havronya Ivanovna to come here!"

A moment later, a loud grunting was heard. Kashtanka growled, put on a brave expression, and moved closer to the stranger, just in case. The door opened and an old woman looked in, muttered something, and let in a very ugly black pig. Paying no attention at all to Kashtanka's growling, the pig raised her snout and grunted happily. She seemed very pleased to see her master, Ivan, and the cat. She came up to the cat and gently rolled him on his stomach with her snout, then struck up a conversation with the goose. Her movements, her voice, and the quivering of her tail expressed nothing but good nature. Kashtanka quickly realized that it was useless to growl and bark at such a character.

23

The master took away the sawhorse and shouted, "Fyodor, front and center!"

The cat got up, stretched lazily, and, as if doing a great favor, went over to the pig.

"We'll start with the Egyptian Pyramid," said the master.

He spent a long time explaining something, then gave the command, "One . . . two . . . three!" At the word "three," Ivan flapped his wings and jumped up onto the pig's bristly back, steadying himself by balancing with his wings and neck. Fyodor, with an air of obvious disdain for his art, climbed reluctantly up onto the goose and stood on his hind legs. The result was what the stranger called the "Egyptian Pyramid." Kashtanka yapped with delight, but at that moment the old tomcat yawned, lost his balance, and tumbled off the goose. Ivan wobbled and fell off, too. The stranger yelled, waved his arms, and began explaining again. After working for a whole hour on the pyramid, the untiring master began teaching Ivan to ride the cat, then he started teaching the cat to smoke, and so on.

At last, the stranger mopped his brow and went out. The lessons were over. Fyodor sniffed scornfully, lay down on his mat, and closed his eyes. Ivan went to the trough, and the pig was led away by the old woman. The day was so full of new impressions that Kashtanka did not notice where the time went. In the evening, she and her mattress were moved into the room with the dirty wallpaper, where she spent the night in the company of Fyodor and the goose.

25

## v. *Talent! Talent!*

A month went by.

Kashtanka was already used to having a nice dinner every evening and to being called Auntie. She was used to the stranger and to her new companions. Life went on smoothly and comfortably.

Each day began in the same way. Ivan usually woke up first, and he immediately went over to Auntie or the cat, bent his neck, and began talking urgently and persuasively, but, as ever, nonsensically. Sometimes he held his head high and delivered a long monologue. At first, Kashtanka thought he talked so much because he was very smart, but after a while she lost all respect for him. When he came up to her with his endless speeches, she no longer wagged her tail but treated him as an annoying babbler who wouldn't let anyone sleep, and answered him unceremoniously with a "grrr. . . !"

Fyodor, however, was a gentleman of a very different sort. When he woke up, he didn't make any noise, he didn't move, he didn't even open his eyes. He would have been glad not to wake up at all, for he obviously didn't like life very much. Nothing interested him, he despised everything, and he even turned up his nose at his delicious dinners.

The master slept late, had his tea, and immediately started working on his tricks. Every day the sawhorse, the whip, and the hoops were brought into the room, and every day almost the same things were repeated. The lessons lasted for three or four hours and sometimes left Fyodor so exhausted he staggered like a drunken man, while Ivan opened his beak and gasped for breath and the master got red in the face and couldn't mop the sweat from his brow fast enough.

Lessons and dinner made the days interesting, but the evenings were rather boring. Usually, in the evening, the master went out somewhere and took the goose and the cat with him. Left alone, Auntie would lie down on her mattress, feeling sad. . . . Melancholy would fall upon her gradually, much as darkness falls upon a room. She would lose all desire to bark, to eat, to run through the rooms, or even to go exploring. Then two vague figures would appear in her imagination. She was unsure if they were dogs or people, but when they appeared, Auntie began wagging her tail, and it seemed to her that somewhere, sometime, she had known and loved them. . . . And each time, as she was falling asleep, these figures brought to mind the smell of glue, wood shavings, and varnish.

But gradually, as she became accustomed to her new life, Kashtanka turned from a skinny, bony mutt into a sleek, well-cared-for dog. One day, her master came to her, stroked her and said, "Auntie, it's time you got to work. Enough of this sitting around. I want to make an artiste out of you. . . . Would you like to be an artiste?"

And he began teaching her all sorts of things. The first lesson she learned was to stand and walk on her hind legs, which she enjoyed greatly. For the second lesson, she had to jump on her hind legs and catch a piece of sugar that her teacher held high above her head. In the lessons that followed, she danced, ran on the tether, howled to music, rang the bell, and fired the pistol. In a month she could successfully take Fyodor's place in the "Egyptian Pyramid." She was an eager student and was so pleased with her own achievements that she

27

followed each successful trick with a joyful yapping. Her teacher was surprised and delighted.

"Talent! Talent!" he said, rubbing his hands. "Real talent! You're sure to be a success!"

And Auntie got so used to the word "talent" that she jumped up each time her master said it, and looked around as if he had called her name.

## VI. *A Bad Night*

Auntie had a dog dream one night that a janitor was chasing her with a broom, and she woke up in a fright.

Her little room was quiet, dark, and very stuffy. The fleas were biting. Auntie had never been afraid of the dark before, but now for some reason she was terrified and felt like barking. In the next room, her master sighed loudly. A moment later, the pig grunted in her shed. Then everything was silent again.

It is always pleasant to think of food, so Auntie began thinking about a chicken leg she had stolen from Fyodor that day and hidden in the living room between the cupboard and the wall, where there were many cobwebs and a lot of dust. It might not be a bad idea to go and see if the leg was still there. It was quite possible that her master had found it and eaten it. But she was forbidden to leave the room before morning—that was the rule. Auntie closed her eyes, hoping to fall asleep quickly, because she knew that the sooner one falls asleep the sooner morning comes. All of a sudden she heard a scream close by

29

that made her jump to her feet. It was Ivan, and the cry was not his usual babbling but a wild, strange, piercing shriek, like the noise of a rusty gate opening. Unable to see or understand anything in the darkness, Auntie felt all the more frightened.

A long time passed, as long as it takes to gnaw a good bone, but the scream was not repeated. Auntie gradually began to doze off. She dreamed of two big black dogs who were greedily eating some mash from a basin. It was steaming hot and smelled delicious. Every once in a while they turned around to Auntie, bared their teeth, and snarled, "We won't give you any!" Then a peasant in a sheepskin coat came out and chased them away with a whip. Auntie went over to the basin and started to eat, but no sooner had the man gone than the two black dogs rushed growling at her. Then, suddenly, there was another piercing scream.

"Ka-ghee! Ka-ghee-ghee!"

Auntie woke up, jumped to her feet, and broke into a howling bark. This time it seemed to her that it was not Ivan but someone else, some stranger, who was screaming. The pig grunted again in her shed.

There was the sound of shuffling slippers, and the master came into the room in his robe, carrying a candle. The wavering light danced over the dirty wallpaper and the ceiling and chased away the darkness. Auntie saw that there was no stranger in the room. Ivan was sitting on the floor. He was not asleep. His wings were spread wide, his beak was open, and he looked terribly tired and thirsty. Old Fyodor was not asleep either. He, too, must have been awakened by the scream.

"What's wrong, Ivan?" the master asked the goose. "Are you sick?"

The goose was silent. The master felt his neck, stroked his

31

back, and said, "You're a funny one. You don't sleep yourself, and you won't let anyone else sleep."

He went out, taking the light with him. It was dark again. Auntie was afraid. She imagined again that a stranger was standing in the dark room. And for some reason she thought that something very bad was going to happen that night. Fyodor was restless too. Auntie heard him stirring on his mat, yawning and shaking his head.

Everyone was uneasy and anxious, but why?

"Ka-ghee!" cried Ivan. "Ka-ghee-ghee!"

The door opened again, and the master came in with the candle. The goose was still in the same position, with his beak open and his wings spread. His eyes were shut.

"Ivan!" the master called.

The goose did not move. The master sat down on the floor in front of him, looked at him silently for a moment, and said, "Ivan, what's the matter? Are you dying or something? Ah, now I remember!" he cried, clutching his head. "It's because that horse stepped on you today! My God! My God!"

Auntie did not understand what her master was saying, but the look on his face told her that he, too, expected something very bad to happen.

"He's dying, Auntie!" her master said, clasping his hands. "Yes, yes, he's dying! What are we going to do?"

Pale and disturbed, the master went back to his bedroom, sighing and shaking his head. Auntie dreaded being left in the dark, so she followed him. He sat down on his bed and said several times, "My God! What are we going to do?"

Fyodor, who rarely left his mat, also came into the master's bedroom and began rubbing against his legs.

33

The master took a saucer, poured some water into it, and went back to the goose.

"Drink, Ivan," he said tenderly, setting the saucer down in front of him. "Drink, my dear."

But Ivan did not move or open his eyes. The master brought his head down to the saucer and dipped his beak in the water, but the goose did not drink, he only spread his wings wider and let his head lie in the saucer.

"No, there's nothing we can do," the master sighed. "It's all over. Ivan is gone!" And shining tears ran down his cheeks like raindrops on a windowpane. Not understanding what was wrong, Auntie and Fyodor huddled close to him, staring in horror at the goose.

"Poor Ivan!" said the master. "And I was dreaming of how I'd take you to the country in the spring, and we'd go for a walk in the green grass. My dear friend, what will I do without you?"

Dawn was breaking, and the invisible stranger who had frightened Auntie so much was no longer in the room. When it was already quite light, the janitor came, picked the goose up by the legs, and carried him out. Later, the old woman came and took away the trough.

Auntie went to the living room and looked behind the cupboard. The master hadn't eaten her chicken leg; it was still there, covered with dust and cobwebs. But Auntie didn't even sniff it. She got under the sofa, lay down, and began to whine softly in a thin voice, "Hnnn . . . hnnn . . . hnnn . . ."

35

## VII. *An Unsuccessful Debut*

One evening the master walked into the room with the dirty wallpaper and, rubbing his hands, said, "Well . . ."

Auntie had made a close study of his face and voice during her lessons, and she could tell that he was disturbed, worried, maybe even angry.

"Today I will take Auntie along with Fyodor," he said. "Auntie, you will replace Ivan in the Egyptian Pyramid. Oh, Lord knows we're not ready yet! We need more rehearsals! It will be a disgrace! A failure!"

He went out and came back wearing his fur coat and top hat. He went over to the cat, picked him up by the front legs, and put him inside the fur coat. Fyodor did not even bother to open his eyes.

"Let's go, Auntie," said the master.

Understanding nothing, Auntie wagged her tail and followed him. Soon she was sitting in a sleigh at her master's feet, and heard him say, shivering with cold and worry, "It will be a disgrace! A failure!"

The sleigh pulled up in front of a large, peculiar building that looked like a turned-over soup tureen. The long, wide entrance of the building with its three glass doors was lighted by a dozen bright lanterns. The doors opened with a loud clang and, like mouths, swallowed up the people who were milling around outside. There were many people; horses, too, trotted up to the entrance. But there were no dogs to be seen.

The master picked Auntie up and shoved her under his coat with Fyodor. It was dark and stuffy there, but it was warm.

37

Two green sparks flashed for a second—the cat, disturbed by his neighbor's cold, rough paws, opened his eyes. Auntie licked his ear. Trying to make herself comfortable, she squirmed and accidentally stuck her head out of the fur coat, but at once gave an angry growl and ducked back inside. She thought she had seen a big room full of monsters. Horrible heads peered out from the barricades and bars that lined both sides of the dimly lit room: horses with horns or with enormous ears, and one huge, fat face with a tail where its nose should be and two long gnawed bones sticking out of its mouth.

The cat meowed hoarsely as Auntie pawed him, but at that moment the coat was thrown open, the master said, "Hup!" and Fyodor and Auntie jumped to the floor. Now they were in a small room with gray board walls. The only furniture was a little table with a mirror on it and a stool. And instead of a lamp or a candle, there was a bright, fan-shaped light attached to a little tube in the wall. Fyodor licked his fur where Auntie had roughed it up and went to lie down under the stool.

The master got undressed, his hands still shaking nervously. Then he sat on the stool, looked into the mirror, and started doing the most amazing things to himself. First he put on a wig with a part down the middle and two tufts of hair sticking up like horns. Then he smeared a thick coat of white stuff on his face, and over the white he painted eyebrows, a mustache, and red spots on his cheeks.

But he did not stop there. Having made such a mess of his face, he began getting into an outlandish costume, unlike anything Auntie had ever seen before. Imagine a pair of the baggiest trousers made out of chintz, with a big flowery print such as some people use for curtains or slipcovers. The trousers

39

came up just under his armpits; one leg was brown, the other bright yellow. Having all but disappeared into these trousers, the master then put on a short chintz jacket with a big ruffled collar and a gold star on the back, socks of different colors, and green shoes.

Auntie's eyes and heart were stunned. The white-faced, baggy figure smelled like her master, his voice was her master's familiar voice, yet she had great doubts and almost wanted to back away and bark at this strange, colorful figure. What's more, they were playing horrible music somewhere behind the wall, and every once in a while there was a loud roar. Only Fyodor's calmness reassured her. He was quietly napping under the stool, and didn't open his eyes even when the stool was moved.

A man in a tailcoat and white vest looked into the room and said, "Miss Arabella is just going on. You're next."

The master didn't answer. He took a small suitcase from under the table, sat down, and waited. From his trembling lips and hands one could see that he was nervous, and Auntie could hear him breathing in short gasps.

"Monsieur George, you're on!" someone shouted outside the door. The master stood up, crossed himself three times, took the cat from under the stool, and put him in the suitcase.

"Come, Auntie," he said softly.

Auntie, who had no idea what was happening, went up to him. He kissed her on the head and put her in next to Fyodor. Then it became dark. Auntie stepped all over the cat, and clawed at the sides of the suitcase, but she was so frightened that she couldn't utter a sound. The suitcase rocked and swayed as if it were floating on water. . . .

"It is I!" the master shouted loudly. "It is I!" After this shout, Auntie felt the suitcase hit against something solid and

41

stop swaying. There was a loud, deep roar. It sounded as if someone were being slapped, and someone—probably the fat face with a tail where its nose should be—bellowed and laughed so loudly that the latch on the suitcase rattled. In response to the roar, the master laughed in a high, squeaky voice, not at all the way he laughed at home.

"My friends!" he yelled, trying to outshout the roar. "I've just come from the station. My old granny kicked the bucket and left me all her money! It's here in this suitcase, and it's very heavy! Maybe a million in gold! Ha, ha! Let's have a look. . . !"

The latch clicked. Bright light struck Auntie's eyes. She jumped out of the suitcase and, deafened by the roar, ran around her master as fast as she could go, yelping all the while.

"Well, I'll be!" shouted the master. "It's Uncle Fyodor and my dear little Auntie! Just my luck!"

He fell down on the sand, grabbed Auntie and the cat, and started hugging them. Auntie caught a glimpse of the world around her and froze for a moment in amazement. Then she tore herself out of his arms and, in her excitement, whirled round and round in place like a top. This new world was big and full of bright light, and everywhere she looked from floor to ceiling there were faces, faces, nothing but faces.

"Auntie, allow me to offer you a seat!" the master shouted.

Remembering what that meant, Auntie jumped up on the chair and sat. She looked at her master. His eyes were serious and kind, as usual, but his face was twisted into a wide, frozen grin. He laughed, jumped around, hunched his shoulders, and pretended to be very happy in front of the thousands of faces. Auntie believed in his happiness. Suddenly she felt that those thousands of faces were all looking at her, and she raised her foxlike head and howled joyfully.

43

"Sit there, Auntie," the master said to her, "while Uncle and I dance a bit."

Fyodor danced reluctantly, glumly, and by the twitchings of his tail and whiskers one could see that he deeply despised the crowd, the bright lights, his master, and himself. Having done his part, he yawned and sat down.

"Well, Auntie," said the master, "now you and I will sing a song, and then we'll dance. All right?"

He took a little flute from his pocket and started playing. Auntie, who couldn't stand music, fidgeted on her chair and howled. Roars and applause came from all sides. The master bowed, and when things quieted down, he continued playing. . . . Just as he hit a very high note, someone high up in the audience gasped loudly.

"Daddy!" a child's voice cried. "Look, it's Kashtanka!"

"You're right!" confirmed a cracked, drunken tenor voice. "It's Kashtanka, Fedyushka, so help me God!"

A whistle came from the top row, and two voices, one a boy's and the other a man's, called out, "Kashtanka! Kashtanka!"

Auntie was startled, and looked in the direction of the voices. Two faces—one hairy and grinning and the other chubby, pink-cheeked, and frightened—struck her eyes as the bright light had done earlier. . . . She remembered. She fell off the chair, floundered in the sand, jumped up, and with a joyful yelp ran toward those faces. There was a deafening roar, pierced by whistles and the shrill shout of a child, "Kashtanka! Kashtanka!"

Auntie jumped over a barricade, then over someone's shoulder, and landed in a box seat. To get to the next tier, she

45

had to leap a high wall. She leaped, but not high enough, and slid back down the wall. Then she was picked up and passed from hand to hand, she licked hands and faces, she kept getting higher and higher, and at last she reached the top row. . . .

Half an hour later, Kashtanka was walking down the street, following the people who smelled of glue and varnish. Luka Alexandritch staggered as he went, and instinctively kept as far as possible from the gutter.

"I'm a sinner! Oh, what a sinner I am. . . !" he muttered. "And you, Kashtanka, are a bewilderment. Compared to a man, you're like a carpenter compared to a cabinetmaker."

Fedyushka walked beside him wearing his father's cap. Kashtanka watched their backs, and it seemed to her that she had been happily following them all this time, and that her life had not been interrupted for a single moment.

She remembered the little room with dirty wallpaper, the goose, Fyodor, the tasty dinners, the lessons, the circus, but it all now seemed to her like a long, confused dream.